E
Rau

Adventurers

Explore in a **Cave**

by Dana Meachen Rau

Photographs by Romie Flanagan

THE ROURKE PRESS
Vero Beach, Florida

For Alice and Romie.

—D. M. R.

Thanks to the Jiganti family and the Chicago Zoological Society/Brookfield Zoo for assisting us in the production of this book.

Photographs ©: Flanagan Publishing Services/Romie Flanagan

An Editorial Directions Book

Book design and production by Ox and Company

Library of Congress Cataloging-in-Publication Data

Rau, Dana Meachen, 1971-
  Explore in a cave / Dana Meachen Rau.
    p. cm. — (The adventurers)
  Includes index.
  Summary: Exploring a cave involves watching hanging bats, following a stream, and looking for paintings.
    ISBN 1-57103-318-1
    [1. Caves—Fiction.] I. Title.

PZ7.R193975 Ex 2000   99-086665
[E]—dc21
© 2000 The Rourke Press, Inc.

Printed in the United States of America.

Are you ready for an adventure?

There are many things to see and do when you explore in a cave!

Hard hat.

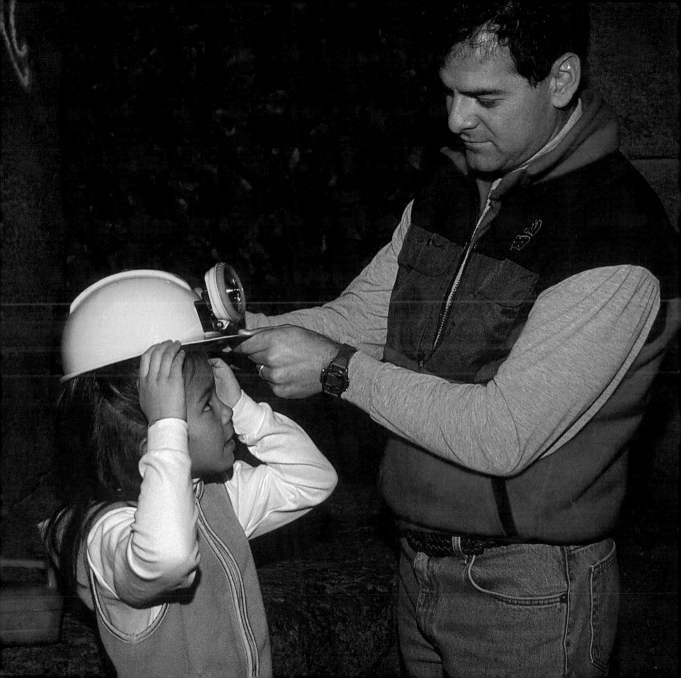

Bright flashlight.

Warm jacket.

That's what I *wear* when
I explore in a cave.

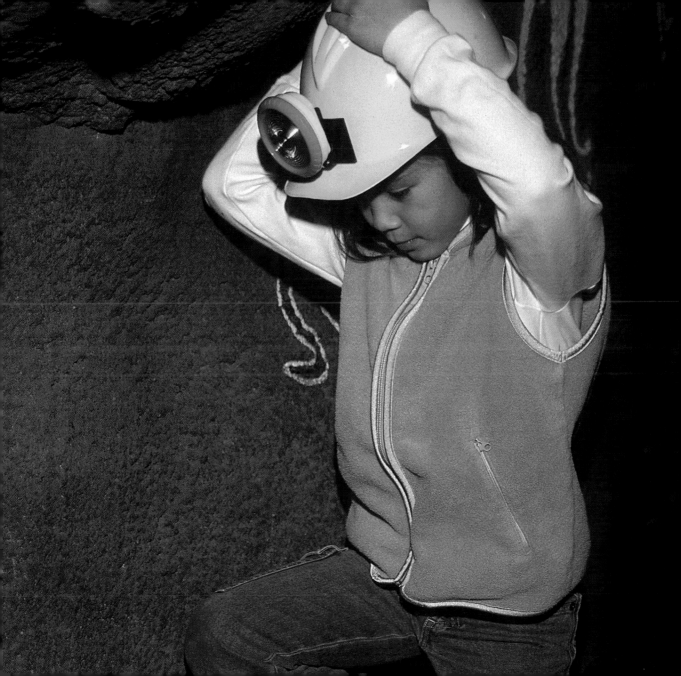

Hanging bats.

Dripping water.

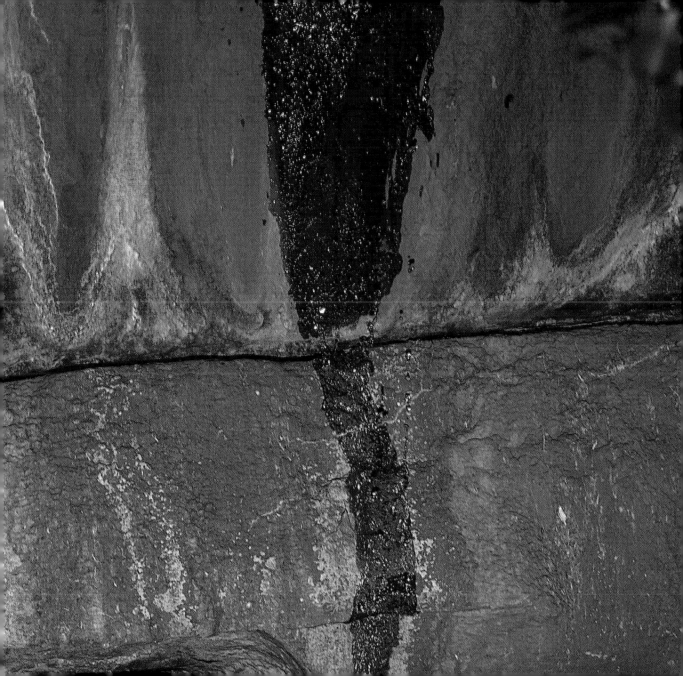

Stone walls.

That's what I *see* when
I explore in a cave.

Follow a stream.

Look for paintings.

Search in the dark.

That's what I **do** when
I explore in a cave.

More Information about Caves

A cave is a large open space under the ground. Caves are created by water carving through the rocks. They are dark and cold. The animals that live inside caves are adapted to life in the dark. People used to live in caves a long time ago. Some of them painted pictures on the cave walls.

To Find Out More about Your Environment

Books

Davis, Wendy. *Limestone Cave.* Danbury, Conn.: Children's Press, 1997.

Fowler, Allan. *Animals under the Ground.* Danbury, Conn.: Children's Press, 1997.

Greenaway, Frank. *Cave Life.* New York: Dorling Kindersley, Inc., 1993.

Web Sites

National Caves Association
http://cavern.com
This site tells you all about caves and where to visit them across the United States.

The National Speleological Society
http://www.caves.org
Visit this site to find out about the National Speleological Society, which studies and explores caves.

About the Author

When Dana Meachen Rau was a child, she and her mother often walked in the woods and splashed in ponds to find the creatures hiding there. Dana loved to write down her thoughts and draw pictures to remember her outdoor adventures. Today, Dana is a children's book editor and illustrator and has authored more than thirty books for children. She takes adventures with her husband, Chris, and son, Charlie, in Farmington, Connecticut.